Phoebe G. Green

Cooking Club Chaos!

Phoebe G. Green

Cooking Club Chaos!

VEERA HiRANANDANi
illustrated by CHRISTINE ALMEDA

PENGUIN WORKSHOP

PENGUIN WORKSHOP

An Imprint of Penguin Random House LLC, New York

Penguin supports copyright. Copyright fuels creativity, encourages diverse voices, promotes free speech, and creates a vibrant culture. Thank you for buying an authorized edition of this book and for complying with copyright laws by not reproducing, scanning, or distributing any part of it in any form without permission. You are supporting writers and allowing Penguin to continue to publish books for every reader.

Text copyright © 2015 by Veera Hiranandani. Illustrations copyright © 2021 by Penguin Random House LLC. All rights reserved. First published in 2015 by Grosset & Dunlap. This edition published in 2021 by Penguin Workshop, an imprint of Penguin Random House LLC, New York. PENGUIN and PENGUIN WORKSHOP are trademarks of Penguin Books Ltd, and the W colophon is a registered trademark of Penguin Random House LLC. Printed in the USA.

Visit us online at www.penguinrandomhouse.com.

Library of Congress Control Number: 2015010133

ISBN 9780593096956 (paperback)   10 9 8 7 6 5 4 3 2 1
ISBN 9780593096963 (library binding)   10 9 8 7 6 5 4 3 2 1

For **Hannah and Eli,**
my favorite foodies
—VH

For **Lola**
—CA

Chapter One

Did you know my middle name is Gertrude, after my great-grandma Gertrude? That's what the *G* stands for. My mom told me Great-Grandma Gertrude really liked to cook and eat, which makes sense, because I do, too. I even found out I'm a foodie, which is someone who loves to eat interesting foods. I don't know if they called people foodies in the very old-fashioned days, though.

Great-Grandma Gertrude grew up in Russia and made things like matzo ball soup (chicken soup with yummy balls made out of matzo stuff), kasha (it's sort of like rice but browner), and knishes (mashed potatoes wrapped up all comfy in dough). She even made her own pickles and kept them in a barrel in her backyard.

Mom always says Great-Grandma Gertrude could cook like nobody's business. But if Great-Grandma Gertrude cooked like nobody's business, how did anyone taste her food? Sometimes things adults say make no sense to me. Actually, there's a lot that doesn't make

sense to me. I like making lists, so
I thought I'd make a list of nonsensey
things:

1. Three weeks ago,
   Sage (one of my
   best friends)
   decided he
   didn't like the
   hot lunch in the
   cafeteria because
   it was too boring (it is). But
   now he brings the same exact
   lunch from home every day.
   Isn't that even more boring?
2. Camille (my other best friend,

who is from France)
always wears fancy
dresses. I think it
might be because
she's French. But
then she can't hang
on the monkey bars
with me and Sage and
that makes her sad. I don't
get why she won't just wear
pants.

❸ Mrs. B, my teacher and the
best teacher ever, got new
glasses that hang on a pretty
chain around her neck. She
used to wear her glasses a lot,

but since she got the new ones I've nEVER seen her put them  on her face. It's a big mystery.

I wonder if I'll ever understand these things. But back to Sage. This is what he brings to lunch every day:

❶ A turkey sandwich: two pieces of turkey, two pieces of bread, and that's it.

❷ A cheese stick (the really bendy kind).

③ A bag of popcorn. (Sometimes when no one's looking, he throws pieces of popcorn at somebody and then pretends he didn't. But I always see him.)

④ An apple (that he doesn't eat at all).

⑤ A box of juice (that he spills on his shirt every time he opens it).

I think it's a perfectly good lunch for one day, but not for the rest of your life. There's just too much good food out there in the world.

Yesterday at lunch while I was eating a salad I made myself (with black beans, corn, tomatoes, and cheddar cheese), and Camille was eating roast chicken with asparagus and a tiny loaf of bread with delicious cheese from a goat, I asked Sage if he was ever going to bring something different to lunch.

He looked at me and blinked. "Why?" he said.

"Don't you get tired of eating the same thing every day?" I asked.

"Why would I? It's my favorite lunch," he said.

It was much worse than I thought. I know this sounds a little weird, but I just couldn't help feeling sad about all the foods he might never eat. Sage didn't like to share lunches with me or Camille, and lunchtime just wasn't as much fun when Sage ate the same thing every day. After school I thought about it and thought about it, but I could only come up with the first part of a plan to help Sage.

It started by wearing a dress to school—my lucky purple one with white and green polka dots on it. I

usually only wear
dresses on picture
day because Mom
makes me.
At breakfast,
everyone noticed.

"What's the
occasion?" Dad
said, drinking his coffee.

"Yeah," my big sister, Molly, said.
"Is it picture day?"

"That's what I was wondering,"
Mom said. "Did I fill out the form? I
don't remember seeing one."

"Hold all of your horses," I said,
holding my fork up into the air. That's

what Dad always says when Molly or
I get upset about something.

Mom, Dad, and Molly looked at me.

"Don't worry, it's part of my plan," I

said, and started

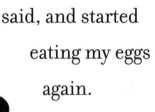

eating my eggs

again.

"Oh, and

what plan is

that?" Mom

asked, the corners of

her mouth smiling in a nervous way.

"Well, I'm afraid Sage is going to eat

the same boring lunch for the rest of

his life and it's not going to be very fun

for him or me. So if I wear a dress,

then he won't think it's strange that I don't want to hang on the monkey bars with him at recess. That way I can talk to Camille in private about what to do, because she always wears dresses," I explained.

"Well, that makes total sense," Molly said, shaking her head, and went off to get her backpack.

"Phoebe," Dad said, putting on his jacket. "Why can't Sage eat whatever lunch he likes?"

"He can, but once a week, tops," I said and crossed my arms.

"Pheebs, just because you like all sorts of things doesn't mean other

people have to as well," Dad said in an extra-nice way. He always does that when he wants to make sure I'll listen.

"Yes honey, you need to let Sage eat what he wants," Mom said, nodding at Dad.

"Okay," I said and smiled weakly. But deep inside my stomach where my scrambled eggs were, I didn't think it was okay. Camille would know what to do. She even liked to eat snails. I saw her do it with my own eyes when we went to France together.

Chapter Two

Later that day on the playground,
I waited for Sage to go off with his
friend Will.

I already told
Sage that there
would be no
hanging on the
monkey bars for
me because of
my dress.

"You look nice, Phoebe," Camille said to me as we looked for sparkly rocks. Camille always spotted the best ones. I liked to look for sparkly rocks almost as much as playing on the monkey bars.

"Do I look French?" I asked, twirling around in my dress.

Camille looked at me in a serious way. "Not really, but you should still wear more dresses. They look pretty on you."

"But then I can't play on the monkey bars," I said really slowly, hoping she would get that the more dresses you wear, the less you play on the monkey bars.

"But I like dresses," she said, staring at me with her big eyelashy eyes.

"Can I tell you a secret?" I asked because she just wasn't getting the whole dress/monkey bar thing.

"Oh, yes," Camille said, nodding fast. "I love secrets. Even more than dresses."

"Okay, but it's a very secret kind of secret," I said.

She nodded extra hard and pressed her lips together.

"I think Sage might have a terrible problem," I said quietly.

She gasped.

"What? What's wrong with him?"

"Well, I think we can help if we do it fast," I said.

"Is he sick? Did he get in trouble?" she said in a worried voice. Camille can get worried very fast.

"I think . . ." I paused and paced back and forth a little. "I think he's going to spend his whole entire life eating the same lunch every day."

Camille let her breath out. "You scared me, Phoebe! That is not a terrible problem." She looked a little mad and Camille usually doesn't ever look mad.

"You don't think so? But you're the least pickiest eater on the planet!" I yelled. "I've seen you eat ducks and snails and cheese with blue polka dots in it and buttery lettuce. You even told me you once ate rabbit stew."

"There are things I don't like," she said, smoothing out her skirt even though it was already smooth.

"I don't believe you," I said, shaking my head. "Tell me one thing you don't like."

She thought for a second. "Raisins. I don't like raisins."

"Well, that doesn't count. Nobody *really* likes raisins."

"They don't?" she asked, squinting her eyes.

I thought about it a bit more. "Okay, forget about the raisins. Let's just think of a plan, because if I have to watch Sage eat one more plain turkey sandwich, it's going to make me too sad for him."

Camille nodded. "Okay, let's think," she said, sitting down on a bench. I sat down next to her and we thought until my head hurt a little.

"I have an idea," she said in her French-sounding movie-star voice.

Camille was very good at ideas. "Sage needs to learn how to cook! Then he'll like more foods."

It was true. I was always extra excited to eat something I helped cook.

"Maybe we could start a club," I said. "A cooking club. Then Sage will get to cook all sorts of foods and he'll try new ones!" I'm pretty good at ideas, too.

"Perfect!" Camille said, and we held each other's hands and jumped up and down because that's what best friends do when they're excited about something.

"Why are you guys so happy?" Sage said, coming over with Will.

I told them about starting a cooking club while still holding Camille's hands and jumping up and down, but of course I couldn't tell him why we had this idea.

"You guys could join," Camille said, and looked at me in the secret part of her eye.

Sage wrinkled his nose. "I don't know. I'm not really into cooking."

I sighed at him and he shrugged and then I sighed one more time and he shrugged again. I was about to do the biggest sigh I could back at him, but

Will interrupted us.

"I like cooking. I'll join!" he said.

"Okay, good. At least someone is excited about our club," I said, and gave Sage a big old eye roll just like Molly does to me when I'm doing things that annoy her.

"Okay, fine," Sage said, this time sighing at me. "I'll join." Then we all started jumping up and down and other kids asked us what was happening, so we told everyone about our idea.

By the time we were back in class, lots of kids were talking about the club and asking if they could join.

"I want to join!" said Grace Wong, leaning toward my desk.

"Me too!" said Miguel Ruiz. "But what kind of club is it?" he asked.

I took a very big breath at him and bonked my forehead with my hand. "You want to join but you don't even know what it is?" I asked.

"It's a cooking club," Charlotte Hempler chimed in. "But who's going to do the cooking?"

"Well everyone, I guess," I said and looked at Camille. We hadn't really thought about that part.

"Where is it going to be?" Grace wanted to know.

"Well, um, we still have to figure that out," Camille said, starting to look a little worried again.

Then more kids started asking more questions and more questions until I began to wonder if this was a good idea after all.

"Hold all of your horses in here!" I yelled, and everyone stopped talking. "Only five people can join," I blurted out. "That's all we have room for, sorry." I hoped that would quiet people down, but it just made everyone louder and kind of mad.

"Whoa." Mrs. B came over to me. "Everything okay, Phoebe?" She played with her glasses on her chain, but did not put them on.

"Well," I said. See, what's great about Mrs. B is that she always listens in a very careful way, and doesn't talk until you're done talking. I wish all grown-ups did that. "Camille and I want to start a cooking club," I said, looking at Camille. "But now everyone wants to join and we can't fit all these people," I continued, pointing at all the kids in my class.

"My, my, you had me a little scared there. But this seems like a fixable problem. Camille, do you agree with

what Phoebe said?" Mrs. B asked.

"Yes," Camille said quietly. She didn't like talking in front of bunches of people. Then this crazy thing happened:

① Mrs. B said, "Hmmm," still fiddling with her glasses.

② She looked up like she was thinking really hard and said, "Huh."

③ The whole class got quiet because they were wondering what she would say after all her hmmm-ing and huh-ing.

④ Then she said, "Let me check

something," and went to her desk and picked up a piece of paper and read it.

5 Then she PUT ON HER NEW GLASSES for the first time and looked at the paper again!

I knew something was special about this day. Maybe it was good luck.

"Phoebe and Camille," she said, taking her glasses off. "You've just given me a great idea."

Chapter Three

When I got home, I couldn't wait to tell my family the big news.

"Mom!" I yelled as soon as I got home. "Something happened!"

Mom came running to the door extra fast.

"What?" she said, a little out of breath. "What is it?"

I puffed out my chest in a very proud way. "I invented a cooking class," I said.

Mom's shoulders fell. "You scared me! I thought something bad happened."

I don't know why, but I seemed to be scaring a lot of people today.

"Well, at first I thought it was bad, but Mrs. B made it good," I said.

"What are you talking about?" Mom asked.

"I think I might need a snack first. I'm running on fumes," I said. I don't know exactly what fumes are, but Mom always says that when she's really tired or really hungry and I was both.

"Okay, Pheebs," Mom said, smiling. We went into the kitchen and she set to work making me one of her yummy snacks. Mom doesn't cook a lot but she makes great snacks. This time it was cracker sandwiches with hummus, tomatoes, and cucumbers inside— creamy, salty, and crunchy all at once.

"So we told Mrs. B about the club

idea," I finished telling her. "And she said a cooking class would be perfect for the after-school program. We can have five classes and a party at the end. We'll learn about a different style of food in each class. Sage said his mom would probably like to teach an Indian cooking class. And Camille said her dad could teach a fancy French dessert class, but we don't know who else can teach yet."

"Sounds like a great idea, Phoebe," Mom said, giving me a big smile, but then her mouth turned into a straight line again. "Wait, are you doing this just because of what you said about

Sage?" she asked.

I bit my lip. I was
and I wasn't. Even if
the cooking club
wasn't part of the
Sage plan, I'd still

want to do it, but I knew if Mom and Dad
thought I was just doing it for Sage, it
probably wouldn't happen.

"Of course not," I said, not quite
looking at Mom's face.

"Phoebe," Mom said. "Look at me."

I looked her right smack in the eye.

"Are you?" she asked. "Tell me the
truth."

I hated when Mom asked me to tell her

the truth. It made me extra nervous. "At first, that was the reason, but now I just want to do it because it'll be so much fun," I told Mom, trying to give her a very not-nervous smile. And it was mostly all true, sort of.

"It is a great idea," she finally said. I looked away as fast as I could.

"What's a great idea?" Molly said, coming into the kitchen. She dropped her backpack at the door and sat on a stool next to me. I told her the whole story, except I left out the Sage part.

"Cool," Molly said. "Maybe Dad could do one," she suggested.

"You mean *our* dad?" I asked, my eyes big.

"Why not?" Molly said, smiling.

I didn't even think about that. Dad and I did more cooking than Mom, but we just made stuff up together, or we followed recipes very carefully. Also, Dad was kind of messy in the kitchen.

"I don't know," I said.

"Dad's on a really busy schedule right now. I don't know if he could get off work," Mom said.

"Then you could do one!" Molly said brightly to Mom. Mom worked at home, so she came to more school stuff.

"Me?" Mom said with a surprised look on her face. "You know I'm not much of a cook, honey. Unless the kids want to learn how to heat up rotisserie chicken."

Molly looked up for a second and tapped her finger on her lips, which meant she was thinking extra hard.

"Actually, you do cook one thing really well," she finally said. "Matzo ball soup!"

"Yeah, Mom!" I said. She did make yummy matzo ball

soup a few times a year on the Jewish holidays. "See, you're almost a good cook!" I said.

"Gee, thanks," Mom replied.

"But is that a *whole* style of cooking?" I said, spreading my arms out wide.

"I think so," Molly said. "Jewish grandmother style!"

Mom got a way-far-away look in her eye. "Your great-grandma Gertrude taught the recipe to my mom, your grandma. Then my mom taught it to me. So I guess it is time I taught you, Phoebe," she said, squeezing my shoulder.

37

"So does that mean you'll do it?" I asked.

"Sign me up!" Mom said.

At first a big happy feeling filled me right up, but then a second later I had my own worried feeling that pushed the happy feeling out. Could Mom actually teach people how to cook something, even if it was matzo ball soup? What was I getting myself into?

By the next week, enough parents signed up for our cooking club and the plan was on its way. Here's who was going to cook with us:

1 Camille's dad was going to teach us how to make chocolate mousse, which is one of the fluffiest, creamiest French desserts ever invented. I tasted it when I went with Camille to France for vacation, so I'm kind of an expert.

2 Sage's mom was going to make something Indian, probably

samosas, which are salty potato-y fried things of yumminess.

3 Grace Wong's mom was going to teach us something Chinese. I kept whispering, "I love beef with broccoli," when Grace was near me so she'd get the idea to ask her mom to make that.

4 Miguel Ruiz's dad was going to do Mexican enchiladas. Miguel told me enchiladas were a little like burritos and a little like fajitas but not like those things at all. So now I have no idea what they are.

5 And my mom was going to make Jewish Grandmother Matzo Ball Soup, which hopefully would turn out okay.

Chapter Four

We had to wait three weeks for the cooking class to start, which felt like forever. Lunches were the worst. I had to watch Sage eat the same stuff over and over and over until it made my head hurt. I decided to write a list about the only foods Sage liked. Then I felt a tiny bit

better because at least I got to make a
list about it:

1 Hot dogs without anything on them

2 Pasta without anything on it

3 Pizza with just cheese on it

4 Turkey sandwiches without anything on them except extra turkey

5 Popcorn with butter on it

6 Cheese sticks — the really bendy kind

POP CORN

43

 **7** His mom's homemade samosas

That's it. Well, he also loves desserts, but who doesn't like desserts? Except he says he doesn't like chocolate, but I don't believe him, because not liking chocolate is basically impossible. And anyway, I knew that once Sage started cooking, everything would change.

Finally, it was the first day of cooking class. We all sat at a table in the cafeteria. Mrs. B got us special, and possibly top secret, permission to use the school kitchen, which was pretty exciting because I had never actually been on the inside of the cafeteria kitchen. After everyone got there, Mrs. B introduced Mr. Durand, who was standing next to Camille.

"Hello, everyone. Welcome to cooking club. Many thanks to Phoebe and Camille for giving us such a great

idea and to Mr. Durand for coming today! Mr. Durand is a professional pastry chef and we are very lucky to have him here. He's going to show us how to make chocolate mousse!"

I smiled extra proudly and looked at Camille. I had made chocolate croissants in Mr. Durand's old bakery in France when we went there on vacation, so I knew all about being a pastry chef. Camille was smiling too, but her cheeks were as red as apples.

We followed Mrs. B and Mr. Durand into the kitchen, which was huge. It had four ovens, three sinks, two big metal counters, and a refrigerator that was big

enough to walk inside!

Mr. Durand organized all the tools and ingredients on one of the big metal counters in the center of the kitchen and made us wash our hands. He said all chefs do that before they cook. Then we surrounded him with our very clean hands and stared at things he took out of bags. I saw cartons of cream. Then I saw lots of chocolate bars, eggs, sugar, and vanilla.

"Aren't you excited, Sage?" I whispered. "Chocolate mousse is so delicious!"

Sage just looked at the table with the ingredients and back at me. "I don't really like chocolate, and anyway, I've never had mousse before, so I don't know," he said.

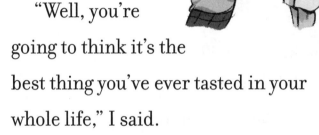

"Well, you're going to think it's the best thing you've ever tasted in your whole life," I said.

But he just shrugged.

Then Mr. Durand passed around the chocolate bars and we got to break them up and put the pieces in a pot. I popped a piece in my mouth. On the wrapper it had said "bittersweet chocolate." It was just that, a little bitter and a little sweet, but I still liked it.

"I saw that, Phoebe." Mr. Durand said, smiling.

I swallowed my chocolate quickly so I didn't have to give it back.

Mr. Durand put the pot of little chocolatey pieces over another pot of boiling water. Camille and I took turns stirring.

"It looks like chocolate soup!" I said when it got all smooth and melty.

After that, Mr. Durand heated some cream in another pot and poured a bit of it into the eggs very slowly as Grace and Miguel took turns mixing.

"If we don't warm up the eggs slowly, we'll have scrambled eggs in our mousse when we cook it all together," he said, which sounded a bit gross.

After that, Charlotte, Sage, and Will stirred the sugar and the eggs and all the hot cream into the hot chocolate

soup and it stayed nice and smooth.
Then everyone got a turn to whip the
rest of the cream. We mixed everything
together and spooned the mixture into
little plastic cups.

"That's it!" said Mr. Durand. "Now we
have to put it in the refrigerator to chill
overnight." Before anyone could say
anything, I gasped.

"What's wrong, Phoebe?" asked
Mrs. B, looking a little scared again.

"We have to wait until tomorrow to
eat it?"

"I don't think I can wait!" Will said.

"Me neither," said Grace Wong.

"*Non*," Mr. Durand said in his serious

French-chef voice and shook his head. "You must let it chill."

I raised my hand slowly, trying to be extra polite.

"Yes, Phoebe?" Mr. Durand said, looking up again.

"But if I really, really wanted to taste it sooner, like maybe right now, would that be, um . . . bad?"

"My dear Phoebe, some things are worth the wait," Mr. Durand explained, and then he winked at me. There was nothing I could do but wink back, but I gave him a really sad wink with a frown.

"Okay, okay," Mr. Durand said. "Everyone can have a taste."

He passed around spoons and we all took a scoop from our cups.

"Whoa!" Miguel Ruiz said after he ate some.

"This might be the best thing I've ever tasted in my life," Will said.

"Yummy, yum, yum!" Grace Wong exclaimed.

Camille smiled and looked at her dad, her face very proud and a little embarrassed.

"Mmmmmmm," I said for an extra-long time as the spoonful of the thick, creamy, warm chocolate melted in my mouth. "Some things are not worth the wait!" Then I turned to Sage. "What do you think, Sage?"

"It's okay," he said, wiping his lips with the back of his hand. "But you know I don't really like chocolate."

I stared at him in disbelief. So did everyone else.

"I never actually *believed* that you didn't like chocolate. I mean WHO DOESN'T LIKE CHOCOLATE?" I shouted at him.

Sage looked at me with a not-so-happy face on. "Me, that's who," he said.

"Phoebe," Mrs. B said. "Everybody has their own taste. There's no right or wrong."

I sat back in my seat and took a deep

breath. "I'm sorry, Sage. I didn't mean to shout," I told him and patted his back. He gave me a weak smile. I was sorry, but I just couldn't understand not loving creamy, freshly made chocolate mousse. Convincing Sage to like new foods was going to be a lot harder than I thought.

Chapter Five

The next week, Grace Wong's mom taught us how to make Chinese pork dumplings. It was kind of like making meatballs, except we wrapped the pork meatball up like a present with a wonton wrapper. Then we cooked them in a big round box that Mrs. Wong called a bamboo steamer.

They tasted salty and gingery.

"This is the best pork meatball present I ever got," I said. Everybody liked them, except Will and you-know-who—Sage. This is what he did:

❶ First he smelled it because he likes to smell things before he eats them.

❷ Then he touched the dumpling to his lips.

❸ Then he smelled it again.

❹ Then I said, "Sage, it won't bite."

 **5** He glared at me but took a little taste and made a face like he just ate a lemon, and put the dumpling down.

"What's wrong?" I asked him, trying to be very calm and sweet so Mrs. B wouldn't get mad at me for not understanding Sage's different tastes.

"I don't know. It's just weird to me. It tastes like soap."

"Your dumpling tastes like soap?" Camille said, looking very confused.

"Soap?" I asked him. "What do you mean?"

"I don't know. Maybe it tastes like hand lotion."

"Hand lotion?" I said, putting my hands on the sides of my face.

"But the dumplings are delicious," Camille said, "and I doubt that hand lotion is delicious."

"My mom has this ginger hand lotion and it smells just like these dumplings," Sage said, pointing at the poor little dumpling sitting on his plate.

Camille and I looked at each other
and shook our heads.

For the third class, Sage's mom, Ramita,
came in. Ramita is from India. She cooks
Indian food in Sage's house, but they also
eat a lot of Italian food, since
Sage's dad is Italian. I guess
that's why Sage likes
pasta and pizza so much.
I've known Ramita
since I was a baby, and
our moms are best friends.
I've eaten a lot of her samosas, but I've
never really watched her make them. It
turns out, making samosas is a little like

making pork dumplings. After we rolled out the dough, we mashed up cooked potatoes and peas and spices, which have beautiful names like turmeric and cumin.

After we spooned all the potato stuff into the dough and wrapped it up, Ramita fried the samosas in a big pot of oil. Then we ate them with a green sauce called chutney. The samosas tasted the way they always taste, a little salty, a little spicy, and crispy delicious.

Sage even had two, but it didn't really count, because they were already on his favorite food list.

The day before the fourth cooking class,
I was hanging upside down on the
monkey bars with Sage and Will, but I
started getting a little dizzy so I went
looking for Camille. She was making a
fairy house out of rocks, sticks, and
leaves on the other side of the
playground. It's a super-special talent

of hers. She says the fairies come at
night to sleep in the
houses. That
can't be true,
but it makes
her happy, so
I don't say a
word about it.

"I really, really hope Sage likes what
we make tomorrow," I said.

"Me too. But what if he doesn't?"
Camille said, looking up from putting a
chunk of moss on her fairy-house roof.

"If he doesn't, then . . . ," I said,
thinking, "then, I don't know."

"Maybe he'll never like trying new

foods," Camille said, looking up.

I thought for a moment. "No," I said. "He will. I think he'll see it'll be more fun if he does."

"I hope you're right," Camille said, and started decorating the front of her house with little pebbles. She suddenly looked up, her eyes all sparkly. "I know! We can write out a wish for the fairies!"

"Huh?" Sometimes Camille got really into her fairy thing.

"If we write a wish for them in the dirt, it might come true."

At this point I was willing to try anything. So we wrote a wish for the fairies in the dirt. We had to call Sage

"S" in case Sage saw it. Our wish said,

Dear Fairies,
Please help S
like more
food.

"There!" Camille said, wiping her

hands on her skirt.

Even if I don't believe in fairies, it

couldn't hurt.

For the fourth class, we made

enchiladas with Miguel's dad. We

stirred around chicken with peppers

and spices in a hot oiled pan and

wrapped them up in cozy corn tortillas.
Then we poured a spicy tomato sauce
over the enchiladas, covered them in
cheese, and put them in the oven.

"It smells like a really good
restaurant in here," I said.

"It does!" Camille said.

Miguel puffed up his chest proudly.

"They're the best enchiladas in the country."

"I don't know about that, Miguel," his dad said, smiling. "But I'll take it."

After they were done, everyone dug in. I looked over at Sage, who sat in front of his enchilada with one small bite taken out of it.

"Why aren't you eating it, Sage?" I asked him, trying not to sound too mad.

"It's too spicy," he said.

"Does it taste like hand lotion again?" Camille said as she licked a bit of sauce off her finger.

"No," Sage said and looked up at the ceiling, thinking. "Just normal spicy, not hand-lotion spicy."

"But you liked your mom's samosas, and *they* were spicy," I said.

"Well, I've been eating them since I was a kid," he said. "I'm used to those spices."

"You're still a kid," I said.

"Then I've been eating them since I was a baby," Sage said.

"You didn't have samosas when you were a little baby," I said.

"How do you know?" Sage replied.

I looked at Camille and she looked

at me and we just shrugged. Once again, our plan was not working. I don't think the fairies read our wish.

"Try tasting it again," Camille told him. "My mom says you taste something the first time to get to know it and then taste it again to become friends with it."

So Sage took another bite. "Still spicy," he said. "I don't think I'm going to be friends with the enchiladas," he said sadly.

I put my head on the table.

"Why do you care so much, anyway?" Sage asked me.

I lifted up my head.

"I don't. I'm just very full," I told him, but I wondered why I did care so much. The truth was, I just wanted him to love trying new foods as much as I did. There were so many exciting foods to try! Was Sage just going to miss out on all that and watch me and Camille have all the fun? I still had one more chance to make the plan work. It was going to be up to Mom and her matzo ball soup.

Chapter Six

On the morning it was Mom's day to make her soup, I started getting butterfly feelings in my belly. That's what Mom and Dad call the jumpy feelings in your belly when you're nervous. They said it doesn't really mean you have butterflies in your belly, but I'm pretty sure I did this time. Maybe I swallowed one overnight.

"Do you have all the ingredients for the soup?" I asked Mom while she drank her coffee.

"I'm getting them later," she said, a sleepy look on her face. Mom's always sleepy until she finishes her coffee. I wanted her to finish it right away so she could get busy thinking about matzo ball soup.

"Did you call Grandma and check the recipe?" I asked. "You don't want to get it wrong."

"I know I'm not a master chef, but

I've been making this soup for twenty years, honey. I could make it in my sleep," Mom said.

"*Sleep?* Mom, you have to make it when you're awake!" I said in a not-so-quiet voice.

"Pheebs," Molly said, laughing. "It's just what people say when they can do something without thinking about it."

"Oh, okay," I said, still wishing her sleepy face would disappear.

"And anyway, Mom said she's making the soup at home and just doing the matzo balls at school," Dad explained as he finished his cereal.

I started to get extra worried now.

"But Mom, all the other parents made their entire recipes at school!" I told her.

"It would take too long to make it all at school, Pheebs," said Mom, taking another too-slow sip.

"Why are you freaking out?" Molly said. She thought everyone was

"freaking out" when they said anything about anything. I think she just liked to say that because it was teenage-y sounding.

"I'm not freaking out. I just want it to be the best matzo ball soup ever made in the whole history of the world," I said. "That's all."

"You've had Mom's matzo ball soup a million times," Molly said. "You know it's delicious."

That was true. It was warm and good smelling, like home in a bowl.

"Thanks, Molly," Mom said.

"I think you might be getting carried away," Dad said, and ruffled my hair as he got up to go to work.

"No one's carrying me anywhere, Dad," I answered. Dad just looked at me funny.

When Molly and I were both zipping up our backpacks in the hallway, Molly whispered to me, "Just make sure Mom doesn't roll the matzo balls too much. I once made them with Grandma and she said that was the trick to keeping them fluffy."

"Got it!" I said and gave her a high five.

After school, Camille and I rushed over to wait for Mom in the cafeteria. We were the first ones there. We sat down, and I couldn't stop tapping my fingers on the table.

"Why are you so jumpy? Are you excited about your mom coming to our club?" Camille asked.

"Yes, I am. I'm very excited, but also calm and not jumpy at all," I said, making a very calm smile at her.

"Okay, because you seem a little bit jumpy," said Camille in her calm French voice.

Then I saw Mom come in with
Mrs. B.

"Hi, Mom," I called as I jumped up
and down, waving. "Do you have all the
ingredients?"

"Wow, Phoebe,
you're especially
excited today," Mrs. B
said.

"I'm very excited and
calm, and not jumpy at all,"
I said, sitting down, looking at Camille.

Camille smiled, but it wasn't her
agreeing-with-me smile. It was a
different kind.

"It's all here." Mom handed me

a bag. She also had two pots. "Why don't you girls bring this stuff into the kitchen and start unpacking?"

I took the bag and Camille followed me.

"All right, I'm jumpy because this is our last chance for the plan to work," I said to Camille now that we were alone. "And to tell you the extra truth, my mom doesn't cook that much."

"I know," she said. "But even if the plan doesn't work, I'm still excited to make matzo balls."

I didn't want to sigh at Camille. But I had to a tiny bit. I started to take stuff out of the bag.

"Phoebe, remember how we decided in France that it was okay for us to be different and still be friends?"

"Yeah?" I said, stopping what I was doing.

"Well, isn't it the same with Sage?" she asked.

I thought about that for a second. "I guess so, but what if we mess up the matzo balls, and Sage decides that he hates cooking and only wants to eat one thing forever? What if that thing is popcorn or something? You can't live on popcorn. This is a food emergency!"

"Gosh," Camille said with her big eyes looking extra worried now. "Do

you think that
could really
happen?"

"It's possible,"
I said, picturing
Sage eating a big plate
of popcorn at the dinner table, everyone
around him trying to get him to taste
other stuff.

Camille's face started to turn a little
pink. "We can't let that happen!" she
said, her French voice getting high-
sounding.

"All I can say is that the soup had
better be good," I said. She nodded very
seriously.

Mrs. B, Mom, and the other kids came in. Mrs. B introduced Mom and explained what we were going to cook. Camille and I went back to unpacking the ingredients on one of the big metal counters. This is what was in the bag:

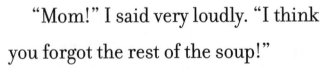

1 Two boxes of matzo meal

2 A carton of eggs

3 A bottle of oil

That's it.

"Mom!" I said very loudly. "I think you forgot the rest of the soup!"

"Phoebe, I told you I made the soup

earlier." She put the pots down on the table. "One pot is the soup. The other is to boil water for the matzo balls."

"Oh, okay," I said, letting out a big breath I didn't know I was holding in. I still wasn't sure Mom could really do this.

"Okay, kids, so let's see," Mom said, putting her glasses on. "First we put the eggs in. Wait, is that right?" she asked, squinting at the matzo-meal box. I thought she could make the matzo balls while she was sleeping, but it looked like she was having trouble making them while she was wide awake. The butterflies in my stomach started flying around again.

All the kids crowded around the table. I chewed a little at my pinkie nail.

"You know what? Let's measure the matzo meal first," Mom said, nodding.

"Who wants to measure?" Everyone shot their hands up in the air.

"Oh my. You all like measuring," she said, smiling at Mrs. B. "Sage, want to give it a try?"

That was good, having Sage do the

first thing. Sage stepped
up and measured out the
cups of matzo meal.
Then Mom let
Grace crack the eggs.
After that, she asked
Camille to put in the water.

"Does Sage want to do it?" Camille
asked, looking nervously at me. "He's
better at it than I am."

"Yeah, Sage is really good at putting
water in things," I said, nodding hard.

Sage stared at me. "Uh, that's okay,"
he said, looking confused.

"I want to give everyone a chance to
help, Pheebs," Mom said and wiped a

stray hair out of her eyes. So Camille
poured in the water. Then she asked
Miguel to put in the oil, and she picked
Will and Charlotte to stir.

I gave her a big frowny face. Mrs. B
came over and bent down toward me.
"I think the best way you can help your
mom is to cheer her on, okay?"

I nodded. I knew how to cheer.
When we used to watch Molly at her
soccer games, I always
cheered the loudest.
Mom started to
show everyone how to
shape the matzo balls.
"Go, Mom, go!" I

yelled. "Go, Mom, go!"

Camille, who was standing next to me, jumped a little. I guess she was feeling a little jumpy too, after all.

"Thank you, Phoebe," Mom said. "But could you be a little quieter, please?"

So I had to whisper-cheer, which doesn't work as well.

"Just roll it into a little ball and drop it into the water," she instructed. Then she gave everyone some batter. I remembered what Molly said about not rolling the matzo balls too much. Grace Wong had been rolling hers for a long time. So had Mom, since she kept showing people with the same matzo ball. Camille was also rolling and rolling.

"Mom." I went over, still whispering. "You have to stop everyone from rolling. The matzo balls won't be fluffy."

"Phoebe, they'll be fine, and it doesn't matter how they come out. It's the experience of making them that counts," Mom whispered back.

"But—" I started to say.

"Honey, I have to work with everyone here," she said. "Go make your matzo balls."

So I watched sadly as all the kids dropped their very rolled matzo balls into the pot of water. As they cooked, Mom explained how she made the soup.

"You put a whole raw chicken in a pot of boiling water," Mom started to explain.

"Poor chicken," Sage said sadly.

Camille and I looked at each other.

"The chicken doesn't know what's happening, Sage," I said.

Camille nodded.

Mom cleared her throat. "Right, um, then you add fresh dill, carrots, onions, celery, and parsnips and simmer for three to four hours," Mom continued.

"Four hours—that's a really long  time," Grace said and crossed her arms over her chest.

Mom wiped her brow and looked at Mrs. B, who gave her a big smile. "Well, after that you take the meat and veggies out and save the chicken broth," she continued slowly.

"Sounds like a lot of work," Will said.

"Yeah," said Sage.

"It's not hard. You just do other things while you wait. My mom makes soup all the time and the house smells so good," Camille said, smiling her sparkly smile. I gave her a thumbs-up.

"I agree. It isn't really that hard," Mom said, but she was kind of making it seem hard.

As it was cooking, the soup started to smell delicious, like I was at my grandma's dining room table. I began to relax a little.

"That does smell good," Sage said.

"It does," Mrs. B said.

"I can't wait to taste it," Grace said.

"Me too," Charlotte said, clasping her hands together.

 Camille and I smiled at each other. Maybe it would turn out well after all.

When the matzo balls were done, we all helped spoon some into the bowls of chicken soup.

"The soup's a little hot, so be careful," Mom said.

I blew and blew on my soup to cool it off. I tried to spoon up a bite of my matzo ball, but the spoon would barely go through. I finally got a piece off and put it in my mouth. It was like biting through a pencil eraser. It was not fluffy at all.

I looked around. Other people were also trying to take spoonfuls.

"This is weird," Grace said, holding up a ball stuck on her spoon.

"Is it supposed to be like this?" Miguel said, also with his spoon stuck. Camille just sipped the soup part in her French movie-star way. I glanced at Mom. Her hair was a little messy, her apron was untied, and her face seemed a bit sweaty. Her eyes caught mine.

"How is it, Phoebe?" she said, wiping the top of her lip with the corner of her apron.

My face felt hot and the tears were starting to come, but I didn't want to make Mom feel bad. I rubbed my eyes a little and took a deep breath. "Well, if the matzo balls were pencil erasers, they'd be really good," I said quietly.

Everyone started to laugh. Mom's face fell.

"Don't laugh at my mom!" I stood up and yelled. That got everyone real quiet.

"Phoebe," Mrs. B said, "please don't yell. But you're right, no one should be laughing."

"Pencil erasers?" Mom said with her worried face on, and she tried to take a bite, but her spoon got stuck, too. "Oh no."

"Maybe people rolled them too much. But it's okay." My voice cracked.
I didn't want Mom to feel bad.

"The soup part is really good!" Camille said extra cheerfully, taking a break from sipping.

"Thanks, Camille," Mom said. "Well, it's the experience, remember?" she said to everyone and reached out to squeeze my shoulder. Except she knocked over the bowl of the leftover matzo balls instead. They went rolling across the table and onto the floor. A few even bounced.

"Oh no!" Mom said.

Everyone jumped up to move away from the matzo balls, and Sage knocked over his soup by accident, which then bumped into Will's bowl and his soup also went splashing onto the floor.

"Uh-oh," said Sage and Will together. Thankfully, the soup wasn't that hot— more like lukewarm.

"I'll get paper towels!" Mrs. B said, running over to the sink. "Let's all help, guys."

Suddenly everyone was running around with pieces of paper towel trying to clean up the mess. I knelt down and picked up a rubbery matzo ball. Camille was next to me sopping up some chicken broth. I looked over at Sage. He was also kneeling on the floor trying to clean up his soup and looking a little mad. This time I didn't blame him. I guess he was doomed to eat nothing but popcorn for the rest

of his whole life and it
was all my fault.

"That was our last
chance," I
murmured to
Camille.

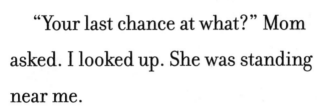

"Your last chance at what?" Mom
asked. I looked up. She was standing
near me.

Camille looked at me with wide eyes.

Before I could say anything, Grace
Wong spoke to me and Mom.

"Don't feel bad. My mom makes
dumplings, like, every week. That's why
she's really good at them," she said.
Sometimes Grace had a way of saying

something not that nice in a really nice way.

"Nothing could ever be as good as that chocolate mousse!" Will said and rubbed his stomach. Camille started to turn red, but a happy red.

"No way," said Miguel. "Enchiladas rule!"

"You're all wrong. The samosas were the best," Sage said.

I didn't say anything. I just went and threw my wet paper towels away.

"Cooking Clubbers!" Mrs. B said in a louder voice than she usually uses. "This is not a cooking contest. It's a cooking *club*, where all foods should be celebrated. Now we've also learned that sometimes cooking

gets a little messy, so let's get this mess
cleaned up like the good chefs we are."

I glanced around. Everyone was on
their knees wiping up cold soup and
rubbery matzo balls. No one looked like
they were celebrating anything. Now
Sage would never like anything new,
especially not matzo ball soup. This was
turning out to be the worst plan I ever
thought of in my life.

Chapter Seven

Mom and I drove back home quietly.

"I'm sorry the soup didn't work out," Mom said after a minute. "I never thought it would be such a disaster. I guess I'm not cut out to teach cooking."

"Even if it went perfectly, I don't know if it would have made a difference," I replied softly.

"Made a difference for what?" Mom

asked in her super-calm voice that she uses when she wants me to tell her the whole story. It all came tumbling out.

"I really wanted Sage to like new foods. Camille and I thought if he learned to cook new things, he'd be all better," I said sadly.

"Better?" Mom asked.

"Remember I told you he has that lunch problem? It's very serious."

"Is that why you wanted to start the club? I thought we talked about this," Mom said in her starting-to-get-angry voice.

"Kind of," I told her in a small voice.

She was quiet for a bit. I could tell she

was thinking. "You know that when you were little you really didn't like peas?" she finally said.

"I didn't?" I said. I liked peas now.

"When we gave them to you, you dumped them right on the floor. You liked lots of things, but not peas."

"Really?" I said. Mom laughed.

"Yes, but I kept making them for you anyway. After a year or two, you would eat a few. And now you like them. It just took time."

"So are you saying that it might be years before Sage wants to eat anything else?" I wailed. "I don't think I can wait that long."

"Just be patient. I was patient with you."

"I'm always patient," I said. Mom looked at me and narrowed her eyes.

"Always?"

"The thing is, Camille and I have so much fun at lunch. I'm worried Sage will feel left out."

"Phoebe, you and Sage have been friends for a long time. Sage having different tastes from you won't change that."

"I hope so," I said. "I just think Sage would like having my tastes even better."

Mom took an extra-deep breath and ran her hand through her messy hair.

Finally, it was lunchtime on the day of the cooking club party. Our parents were bringing another batch of the dishes they made for the class. I was worried that everyone would start arguing again over whose food was the best. I sat back and watched Sage eat his lunch while I ate my cream cheese and smoked salmon sandwich. This is how he ate his lunch:

❶ First he took the crusts off his turkey sandwich.

❷ Then he took six bites of it.

❸ After that, he unwrapped his cheese stick very slowly and peeled off little strips of it, tilted his head back, and dropped them in his mouth.

4 He ate his
popcorn piece
by piece,
sometimes

throwing a piece up in the air
and catching it in his mouth.
5 Then he took out the apple
he never eats, looked at it,
and put it back in his
lunch box.

6 When all the
eating was done,
he opened his juice,
spilled a little on his
shirt, and drank it.

"Look at Sage," I whispered to Camille as I watched him.

She looked at him and then back at me. "Yeah?" she said.

"He really likes his lunch," I told her. "I've never seen anyone look so happy to eat their lunch. I guess I never realized that before."

Camille nodded.

"It looks like he likes his lunch as much as we like ours."

"Yeah, I guess so," Camille said.

"Could that even be possible?" I asked.

"Maybe," she said.

I felt like I was understanding something important. "I guess we should have left him alone about his lunch," I said, looking down.

"Maybe," Camille answered. "I still think he had fun in the club, though."

"I don't know," I said quietly. I wondered if I did something to Sage that I couldn't undo. I suddenly didn't care at all about Sage's tastes. I just wanted to make sure he wasn't mad at me.

Everyone's parents came to the party. Mom had saved the leftover chicken broth from the cooking club in the freezer so she didn't have to make a whole new pot, and the night before the party she let me and Molly make the matzo balls. This time we barely rolled them and hoped for the best.

When Camille, Sage, and I walked into the cafeteria, I stopped and stared. There was a big table in the middle with a white tablecloth on it and little cups of chocolate mousse, a big platter of enchiladas, a tray of dumplings, a tray of samosas, and bowls of soup. "Hold all those horses!" I exclaimed.

Mrs. B and all the parents stopped what they were doing and stared at me.

"Phoebe, what's wrong?" Mom asked.

"Nothing," I said. "All that food just looks so good. It's like a super-fancy party!"

"It is," agreed Mrs. B.

"And it's going a little more smoothly than my cooking class!" Mom said, laughing, and we all laughed.

"Good thing Sage is a picky eater or we would have never come up with this class," Camille whispered in my ear.

I hadn't thought of it like that. Sometimes Camille really did know the best things to say.

I looked across the room and I couldn't believe what I saw. Sage was holding a bowl of matzo ball soup and actually eating it.

"Sage!" I said as Camille and I ran over to him. He jumped, almost spilling his soup. "Are you really eating that?"

"I tasted the soup again and I like it better this time. The matzo balls are soft and fluffy. It's not that bad after all."

"Cool!" I said, beaming, glancing at Camille. Then I looked back at Sage.

"I'm sorry I was upset about your lunches. I won't be anymore."

"Me neither," said Camille.

"Why? Because I'm eating your soup?" he asked.

"No, because your lunches make you happy," I said. "I watched you eat today and I saw that."

Sage smiled *and* shrugged. "Yeah, I guess they do," he said.

"Did I make you feel bad?" I asked him, searching his eyes.

"Well, I didn't like when you got mad at me about the chocolate mousse. But mostly the cooking club was fun. I'm glad you guys thought of it."

"You are?" I said, my smile just about jumping off my face.

"Phoebe, don't get too excited. I think I need a little cooking break."

"Okay, okay," I said.

"And my lunch is pretty good. You guys should try it sometime," he said, grinning at me and Camille.

"I have always wanted to try one of those, what do you call them, sticks of cheese?" Camille said.

"You've never had a cheese stick?" Sage and I said at the same time.

Camille shook her head.

"They're actually pretty good," I said. "Especially the really bendy kind."

"I'll bring extra tomorrow!" Sage said proudly. "One for each of you."

"Thanks," Camille said, turning a little red.

I looked around. Everybody was eating, laughing, and having a good time. It didn't matter what they were eating, just that they were enjoying it.

Camille, Sage, and I walked arm in arm to the food table and piled plates high with dumplings, enchiladas, samosas, and soup. We sat with our friends from the cooking club, and dug into our delicious food. The soup was yummy, and made me think about holidays at my grandma's table. It even made me think about Great-Grandma Gertrude, who probably invented matzo ball soup. That's when I understood the most important thing about food: It isn't about what people eat, but that they share it together.